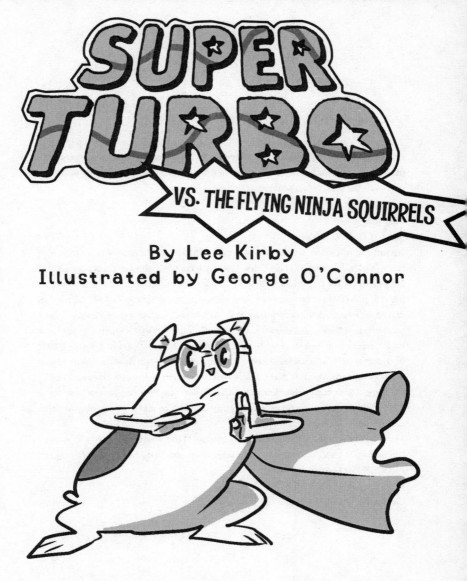

SUPER TURBO

VS. THE FLYING NINJA SQUIRRELS

By Lee Kirby

Illustrated by George O'Connor

LITTLE SIMON

New York   London   Toronto   Sydney   New Delhi

This book is a work of fiction. Any references to historical events, real people, or real places are used fictitiously. Other names, characters, places, and events are products of the author's imagination, and any resemblance to actual events or places or persons, living or dead, is entirely coincidental.

LITTLE SIMON

An imprint of Simon & Schuster Children's Publishing Division • 1230 Avenue of the Americas, New York, New York 10020 • First Little Simon hardcover edition December 2016 • Copyright © 2016 by Simon & Schuster, Inc. All rights reserved, including the right of reproduction in whole or in part in any form. LITTLE SIMON is a registered trademark of Simon & Schuster, Inc., and associated colophon is a trademark of Simon & Schuster, Inc. For information about special discounts for bulk purchases, please contact Simon & Schuster Special Sales at 1-866-506-1949 or business@simonandschuster.com. The Simon & Schuster Speakers Bureau can bring authors to your live event. For more information or to book an event contact the Simon & Schuster Speakers Bureau at 1-866-248-3049 or visit our website at www.simonspeakers.com. Designed by Jay Colvin. The text of this book was set in Little Simon Gazette.

Manufactured in the United States of America 1116 FFG 10 9 8 7 6 5 4 3 2 1

Cataloging-in-Publication Data for this title is available from the Library of Congress.

ISBN 978-1-4814-8888-4 (hc)

ISBN 978-1-4814-8887-7 (pbk)

ISBN 978-1-4814-8889-1 (eBook)

CONTENTS

THE GOLDEN ACORN

Actually, *below* these walls, in the basement. Specifically, in the pantry. Normally, Sunnyview Elementary was filled with kids and teachers and all the things that make up a school. But it was after hours. Everyone was at home or asleep. And not a creature was stirring, except for a— What is that? A mouse?

"Fellow rats!" cried a small, fuzzy creature with huge ears and long whiskers. He addressed a crowd of other creatures just like him. Although he was a bit smaller than

the rest, his whiskers were longer. This is why he was called . . .
Whiskerface!

"I suppose you're all wondering why I called you here tonight!"
Whiskerface continued.

There was a chorus of whispers. "Uh, was today Taco Tuesday?" asked a tiny voice from the back.

"No!" roared Whiskerface. "It's not even Tuesday. It's Friday!

"As you all know, the Rat Pack recently suffered a defeat at the paws of the pampered pets of Sunnyview Elementary." Whiskerface stroked his whiskers as he reminded his Rat Pack what had happened.

A team of classroom pets had showed up in his cafeteria and halted his plan to take over Sunnyview Elementary and, eventually, the world!

"But as your fearless leader, I have taken steps to make sure that the Rat Pack won't be defeated again!" Whiskerface cried.

As he said this, a couple of Rat Packers approached Whiskerface's podium, carrying what looked like a box covered with a blanket. The crowd murmured excitedly.

Whiskerface waited for the sounds to die down. "Have you all heard of . . . the Golden Acorn?!"

THE GOLDEN ACORN?!
THAT'S THE SACRED SYMBOL OF NUTKIN!
NUTKIN AND HER FLYING NINJA SQUIRRELS!

"Exactly!" yelled Whiskerface. "And according to legend, the Golden Acorn gives great strength and speed to its owner! And I . . ." Whiskerface paused dramatically, looking around the room. "I am now in possession of the Golden Acorn!"

The room buzzed. Everyone wanted to know how Whiskerface had stolen the Golden Acorn.

"I defeated the ninja squirrels in combat," Whiskerface declared, describing the epic battle.

"And now I present to you . . .
the Golden Acorn!" Whiskerface
cried. He dramatically pulled off
the blanket.

The room fell silent. Finally, a
voice from the back called out:
"Uh . . . , Whiskerface, sir . . . The
acorn . . . It's—it's not there."

Whiskerface gasped. "It's gone!" he screamed. "Someone has stolen the Golden Acorn . . . again!"

RETURN OF THE SUPERPET SUPERHERO LEAGUE

Meanwhile, in Classroom C of Sunnyview Elementary, Turbo was running his daily laps on his hamster wheel.

Who is Turbo, you ask? Turbo is the official pet of Classroom C. It's a responsibility he takes very seriously. But there is a lot more to Turbo than just that.

You see, Turbo is not just a class-room pet hamster. Turbo is also . . . a superhero! As the heroic Super Turbo, he fights a never-ending battle against evil. And Turbo *him-self* recently learned that he is not alone! All the classroom pets of Sunnyview Elementary are superheroes.

Not very long ago, Super Turbo and the other pets had teamed up to prevent Whiskerface and his Rat Pack from taking over the school and then the world! After that, Super Turbo and his friends had decided to fight evil together. And they would fight it as:

THE SUPERPET SUPERHERO LEAGUE!

Turbo was lost in thought when two faces suddenly appeared at his cage.

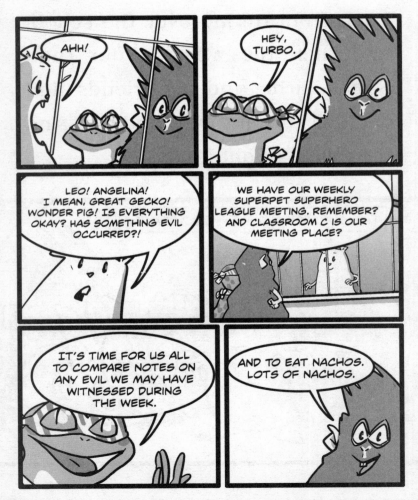

Turbo *hadn't* remembered. But he was excited to see the rest of the team, hear about their solo adventures, and of course, eat some nachos. And it didn't make sense to go to a Superpet Superhero League meeting as plain old Turbo. He would go as . . . Super Turbo!

Super Turbo climbed out of his cage and raced down to the reading nook. That was the meeting place for the Superpet Superhero League.

The Great Gecko and Wonder Pig were already there, of course, and so was Warren, the science lab turtle.

HEY, PROFESSOR TURTLE!

GREETINGS AND SALUTATIONS, SUPER TURBO!

The cover to a vent was resting against the wall. The superpets used the vents as a secret way to travel from room to room in Sunnyview Elementary. Only Wonder Pig, with her amazing maze-running skills, knew where all the vents led.

Suddenly there came a rumbling sound from the vents. Clever, the parakeet from Classroom D—who was also known as the Green Winger—came in, pushing the Turbomobile.

Turbo had generously given his Turbomobile to Nell—also known as Fantastic Fish. That way she could attend meetings and get around the school.

Finally, Frank—also known as Boss Bunny—came hopping in. Now, the superpets were assembled!

The Green Winger thoughtfully took notes as each super-pet detailed their week's adventures. Boss Bunny, the official pet of the principal's office, went first.

Fantastic Fish reported that, from her fish tank in the hallway, she noticed the janitor never locked his closet. That wasn't necessarily evil, but it was something that the superpets could look into.

The Great Gecko mentioned that Classroom A was going on a field trip next Thursday.

Wonder Pig told them how she had snuck into the cafeteria on Taco Tuesday, and that's where she had gotten the nachos. The superpets all clapped for her.

The Green Winger took a break
from writing to report that she had
witnessed no evil, but had perfected

a brand-new acrobatic routine she
was anxious to share with them all.

Super Turbo said that all was safe in Classroom C, though he did note to himself to keep a closer eye on Meredith.

Finally, it was Professor Turtle's turn to speak. Super Turbo leaned back. This would take a while. Everyone loved Professor Turtle, but he *was* a turtle, and sometimes it took him a long time to say things.

Well, that was quick! And almost as quickly, the superpets were headed to the lab!

THINGS GO BOOM!

The superpets raced down the vent, with Professor Turtle leading the way. In fact, Professor Turtle was moving so fast that Super Turbo was having trouble keeping up. Or maybe Super Turbo was moving slower than usual?

Probably shouldn't have had so many nachos, he thought. Then he

noticed that Wonder Pig was strug-
gling to keep up alongside him too.
And so was Boss Bunny.

The superpets exited the vent
onto one of the lab's worktables. A
brown papier-mâché mountain was
resting on the table before them.

The Great Gecko scampered up
the side of the volcano and peered
down the hole. "Hey, there's a soda
bottle in here!" he exclaimed in
surprise.

"Yes!" replied Professor Turtle. "That's where we'll be mixing our own lava! First, we need some water." He glanced at Fantastic Fish.

"Don't look at me," said Fantastic Fish from the Turbomobile. "I need all the water I have."

Super Turbo had an idea. He attached a rubber tube to the end of a faucet, and the Great Gecko ran the other end of the tube to the top of the volcano. Using her super-pig strength, Wonder Pig turned on the faucet to fill the bottle with warm water.

"Now we need to add baking soda!" yelled Professor Turtle.

"We're going to bake a soda?!

Yuck! I prefer my soda cold," said Wonder Pig.

"Not me. I don't even like soda. The bubbles go right up my nose," added Boss Bunny.

"It's too bad someone already emptied this soda bottle if we're going to need to bake it," said the Great Gecko from atop the volcano.

"Are we even allowed to use an oven without supervision?" asked Super Turbo.

Professor Turtle ran over to a box of white powder and stuck in a spoon. "This is baking soda. Green Winger, if you could kindly drop some of this into the volcano?"

The Green Winger flew the baking soda to the top of the volcano. She and the Great Gecko stirred it.

"One final thing!" said Professor Turtle. "Vinegar!"

Wonder Pig and Super Turbo carefully carried a bottle of vinegar up to the top of the volcano. They slowly turned the bottle upside down.

"And now!" yelled Professor Turtle. "Mount Krakabooma erupts!"

Boss Bunny covered his ears. The Green Winger covered her eyes. Fantastic Fish couldn't really cover the Turbomobile. They waited. But nothing happened. And then . . .

"Ha-ha! That was GREAT!" yelled Professor Turtle from on his back.

All the superpets were covered in lava. They agreed they should probably clean up the mess and then head back to their own classrooms to clean up *themselves.*

Just as Super Turbo was about to head back

to Classroom C, a glint of something caught his eye.

"Professor Turtle? What is that in
your cage?" he asked.

"You know, I'm not quite sure,"
said Professor Turtle, removing
his Super Visor. "It's shaped like
an acorn. I found it in the school
cafeteria this morning, and I was
just . . . drawn to it. I've always
liked shiny things."

Super Turbo tried to take a step closer to get a better view, but his paws were stuck to the floor. "Ugh, I better go wash off before I get stuck here forever!" he said. He carefully unstuck each of his paws and scampered down the vent to Classroom C.

4

AN INVISIBLE VISITOR

Safely back in Classroom C, Turbo took a shower in the drinking fountain. Then he cracked open a window to let the wind dry his fur.

It had certainly been an eventful day, even without evil to fight. Turbo was tired and he deserved a nap. But first, he had to do his patrol of Classroom C.

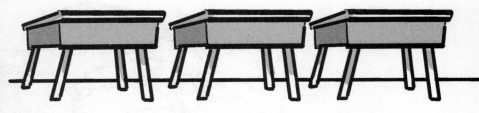

Desks all in a row? Check.

Chalk in the chalkboard holder? Check.

Hamster wheel nice and squeaky? Check.

Supergear safely stashed and drying out? Check.

Well, thought Turbo, clapping his paws together, *looks like it's all clear in Classroom C!*

Turbo pulled out his hammock and settled in. He lay back, and just as his eyes began to close . . .

Turbo sat upright in his hammock.
He could have sworn he saw . . .
something. A shadow. He scanned
the room from his cage. *No, I'm just
tired and my eyes are playing tricks
on me,* he decided. He lay back
down. And then . . .

Again! This time Turbo was sure something was in the classroom with him. He put on his still-damp Super Turbo gear and climbed down from his cage.

Using all of his super-hamster sneakiness, Super Turbo searched the classroom.

There was no sign of any intruder. He must have imagined it all. And now his goggles were fogging up, so he took them off to wipe the lenses with his cape.

Then . . .

What had just happened?! Super
Turbo raced over to the door. He
certainly couldn't open it himself.
But he was sure that someone—or
something—had just gone out it.

"This looks like a bigger mystery
than any *one* superhero can solve!"
Turbo announced.

He ran over to the vents that con-
nected all the superpets' classrooms
to one another. He grabbed the ruler
that lay just inside the vent.

When they had formed the Super-pet Superhero League, the Great Gecko had come up with a secret code the superpets could use to communicate through the vents. Super Turbo tapped the corner of the ruler on the metal floor of the vent. The sound echoed throughout the whole system.

One tap meant: *All's well, nothing to worry about here. Carry on.*

Two taps meant: *Hey, I'm hungry. Who wants to go to the cafeteria for some snacks?*

And three? Three taps meant:

5

SUPERPETS ON PATROL!

The Superpets quickly arrived at Classroom C, ready to fight evil. Surprisingly, Professor Turtle had been first to arrive. He was usually the last, since he moved so slowly. The rest of the team followed him in.

"I'd just emptied out the Turbo-mobile when I heard the call," said Fantastic Fish.

"What's happening, Super Turbo?" asked Wonder Pig. "When I heard the first tap, I was like, oh good, all is well. But then I heard the second tap and I was like, Super Turbo is hungry? We just had nachos! And then I heard the third tap . . ."

"Well, I don't know if it's evil, but something very strange is definitely going on," said Super Turbo. He told the Superpet Superhero League what he had seen . . . or rather, *not* seen.

The Great Gecko stroked his chin. "You were right to sound the alarm, Super Turbo. This is very strange indeed."

"I wonder if the intruder was invisible?" asked Fantastic Fish.

"Or what if it was a g-g-ghost?" stammered Boss Bunny.

The Great Gecko was about to speak again when Professor Turtle said, "The smartest idea will be for us to split up into smaller teams and explore the school. We can cover more ground that way and meet back here in thirty minutes."

The Great Gecko blinked. "Yeah, what Professor Turtle said."

"Okay!" continued Professor Turtle. "Great Gecko: you, Wonder Pig, and Fantastic Fish can check

the hallways. Green Winger: you and Boss Bunny can check the gymnasium. Super Turbo: you and I will cover the cafeteria. Let's go, superpets!"

Everyone was so surprised by Professor Turtle's quick thinking and take-charge attitude that they stood still for a second. But it *was* a good plan, so they sprang into action.

Fantastic Fish knew the hallways the best, so it made a lot of sense for her to cover them. With the Great Gecko and Wonder Pig alongside, they were able to finish their patrol in no time. They didn't see any sign of the invisible intruder, but they did stop to lock the janitor's closet.

Boss Bunny and the Green Winger arrived in the gymnasium. Using his bunny-burrowing powers, Boss Bunny squeezed behind the bleachers to see if there was any sign of the intruder.

The Green Winger flew up to the ceiling to see if a bird's-eye view revealed some evil. They didn't find anything.

Since they had extra time, and all the extra space, the Green Winger decided to show off the new acrobatic move she had perfected: the Triple Loop-de-Loop with an Aerial Twist.

"Brava!" Boss Bunny clapped.

Meanwhile, Super Turbo and Professor Turtle were in the cafeteria. Once again, Super Turbo found he was having a hard time keeping up with Professor Turtle. But now Super Turbo was pretty sure that he wasn't getting *slower*. Professor Turtle was definitely getting *faster*. He seemed to be growing more confident, too. It was like a whole new professor!

The first time Super Turbo had been to the cafeteria was also when he'd had his first clash with evil. He and the superpets had battled Whiskerface and his Rat Pack. There hadn't been a peep from those rodent rascals since then, but Turbo gave a shudder at what a close call their battle had been. And hadn't something else happened recently in the cafeteria too?

The two superheroes completed their sweep of the cafeteria and came up empty-pawed. Nothing suspicious to be found! They headed back to meet up with the others at Classroom C.

A few moments later, two sets of beady yellow eyes peered out of a tiny crack in the cafeteria wall.

"Did you hear that? The turtle found the Golden Acorn!"

"Whiskerface is going to be so pleased when we tell him!"

THIS FIGHT IS TOTALLY NUTS

Back in their meeting spot in the reading nook of Classroom C, the superpets all shared what they found—or rather, didn't find—on their patrols.

Super Turbo walked away from the group and wondered to himself: *Did I actually see anything? Was that really the door opening and closing that I heard? Or was it all in my head?*

Just then, something rattled. It was the doorknob. "Guys! Look!" Super Turbo yelled, pointing.

The superpets froze as the door-knob turned, and the door slowly opened.

"Oh my gosh, they *are* invisible!" yelled Wonder Pig, and she began karate chopping the air all around her.

"They're g-g-ghosts!" shrieked Boss Bunny, and fainted into the Great Gecko's arms.

"Shh! Be quiet and hide!" said Super Turbo.

The superpets all found hiding spots in the bookshelf and waited.

After a few moments, a masked figure dressed all in black crept into the room. It didn't make a noise. It had a huge bushy tail. And it was followed by two identical figures.

Suddenly, Professor Turtle yelled out: "NINJA SQUIRRELS!"

The three Ninja Squirrels snapped to attention and took battle stances.

Their cover blown, the superpets leaped out into their best superhero poses. Suddenly, the Ninja Squirrels launched themselves at the superpets.

"They're not just Ninja Squirrels!" the Green Winger yelled. "They're FLYING Ninja Squirrels!"

The Green Winger flapped into the air as the rest of the superpets dove out of the way of the Flying Ninja Squirrels.

With her supercool Triple Loop-de-Loop with an Aerial Twist maneuver, she was able to make two of the Flying Ninja Squirrels crash into each other.

But on the ground, the squirrels were almost too quick for the eye to follow.

Even the Great Gecko, one of the speedier members of the Superpet Superhero League, was having a

hard time keeping up with the acrobatic Flying Squirrels. Surprisingly,
Professor Turtle, whose normal
fighting technique was to curl up
into his shell, was doing quite well.

The battle raged around Class-room C. Super Turbo climbed up on top of his cage and saw that the room—*his* room!—was getting destroyed! And what sort of official classroom pet would he be if he let that happen?

EVERYBODY STOP!

7

EVERYBODY STOPS

Everyone stopped and looked at Super Turbo.

"This is my classroom," he said. "And you all are really making a mess of it."

The rest of the animals hung their heads, embarrassed.

"We're sorry, Super Turbo," said Wonder Pig. Then she strolled up to the nearest Flying Ninja Squirrel, held out her hand, and said, "Hi, I'm Wonder Pig. Nice to meetcha."

The Flying Ninja Squirrel glanced back to her friends, shrugged, and held out her paw. "I'm Nutkin."

The rest of the superpets and

Flying Ninja Squirrels made intro-
ductions to one another. Super
Turbo was surprised at how polite
the ninjas were. They didn't seem
so evil, after all.

"So what brings
you to Sunnyview
Elementary, Nutkin?"
Super Turbo asked.

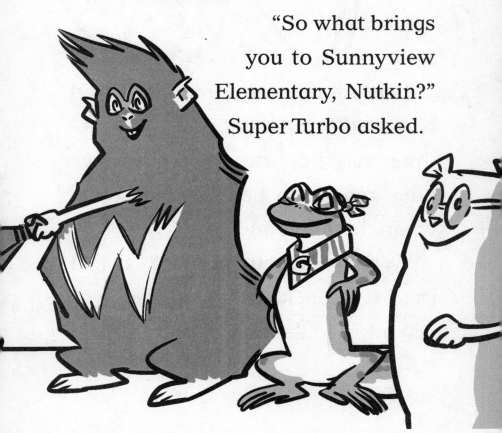

"We are missing something," said Nutkin after a slight pause. "Something very important to us. And we have reason to believe it is somewhere in this school."

"What are you missing?" asked the Great Gecko.

Nutkin looked back and forth to

the other Flying Ninja Squirrels. "This is a very, uh, delicate matter for us. Do you mind if we take a moment to discuss?"

"Take your time," said the Great Gecko, waving his hand. "We have some important matters to discuss as well."

The two groups moved to opposite sides of Classroom C and formed huddles.

Turbo rubbed his hand gingerly. "Wow, you're strong!"

"Of course I'm strong!" she said. "I'm a guinea pig and I have super-pig strength!"

Turbo's mouth fell open. "Super-pig strength?" he asked.

He also noticed that she had a perfect white W in the middle of her fur.

"But that's not my real super-power," Angelina added.

Superpower? What was going on? But before Turbo could respond, Leo jumped between them.

"Ha-ha, that's enough, Angelina," Leo said quickly. "Okay, well, we'll be getting along. Turbo, it was nice to meet you—"

Suddenly something fluttered onto the floor.

"Hey?" said Turbo. "Is that a . . . mask?"

Leo swiftly scooped up the mask and hid it behind his back.

But Angelina said, "It's too late now, Leo. He knows."

Leo turned around. Turbo wondered if he was about to run away. But when Leo turned *back* around, he was wearing the mask and a

supercool handkerchief with a giant
G on it.

Turbo's eyes practically popped
out of his head. Angelina was also
now wearing a mask and the W
on her belly almost seemed to be
glowing.

AND I'M NOT JUST ANGELINA . . .
I'M WONDER PIG!

Turbo looked back and forth
between the two pets. "You! Guys!
Are! Superheroes?!"

Leo nodded. "But this is top
secret information, and you must
promise to keep it that way," he
told Turbo.

Without a word Turbo raced off. Leo and Angelina just looked at each other.

"I guess that was too much for him," said Angelina.

"Well, we are pretty awesome," said Leo.

Suddenly the caped figure leaped back into view.

Now it was Angelina's and Leo's turn to be surprised.

Leo rubbed his eyes. "Another superhero?! This is *great*! Angelina, leave your book here for now. Let's introduce Super Turbo to the team!"

4

MEET THE TEAM!

"Team?" asked Turbo.

Angelina smiled. "There aren't just other classroom *pets*," she said. "There are other pet *superheroes*! I'll show you the way."

The three heroes scampered over to the vent by the door of Classroom C. Angelina lifted the grate off the

vent so
that Turbo
and Leo could get
inside. They followed her down
the length of the duct until they
came to another grate.

"Hiya, Clever!" Leo said with a
wave as he stepped out.

In a cage way above them, a

green parakeet looked down. "Hey, Leo! Hey, Angelina! Who's that with you guys?"

"This is Super Turbo" said Angelina. "He's the pet protector of Classroom C!"

Clever unlocked her cage and flew down to them. The animals all followed Angelina through the vents. They came out into another room, filled with beakers, scales, and microscopes.

"This is the science lab. Warren lives here," explained Angelina.

Clever flew up to a glass case.

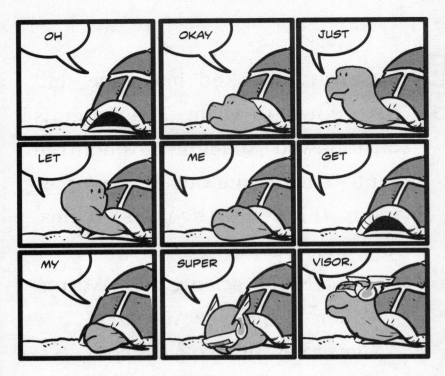

Even with the other animals' help, it still took a very long time to get Warren down to the vents.

"I like your visor," Turbo told Warren.

"Thanks," said Warren. "The . . .

wings . . . make . . . me . . . go . . . faster."

Leo placed his hands where his hips would be if geckos indeed had hips.

5

SOMETHING SMELLS FISHY

PRINCIPAL

Turbo had never been to the principal's office, but he knew from his time in Classroom C that it was a place to be avoided at all costs. Only students who were in the biggest trouble possible went to the principal's office. So what sort of terrifying pet would live there?! The vent in the principal's office was conveniently located right above a shelf. The room was dark as all the animals filed out one by one. Turbo noticed a big cage that was made of wire—like his—and wood.

Suddenly the lights flickered on.

Meanwhile, Angelina had grabbed a rope the pets kept stashed under the garbage can. Like a pro, she swung the rope and lassoed the door handle. Each animal grabbed onto the end, and together they pulled. The doorknob turned . . . and turned . . . and finally . . . *CLICK!* They pulled the door open.

"Wow!" Turbo exclaimed. He was very impressed.

The animals filed out of the principal's office and into the hallway. Suddenly there was a voice.

But how?

The pets all thought hard.

"I could build a teleporting machine," offered up Warren. "We could teleport Nell out of the fish tank!"

"You can do that?" asked Turbo, shocked.

"Well . . . I never have before," admitted Warren. "But I could try."

"Even if we could teleport Nell down here, she would still need water to breathe," Leo pointed out.

"I have an idea! Wonder Pig, come with me!" Turbo pulled his cape tight and scampered down the hall.

Angelina looked to the others, shrugged,

and ran off after him. The other animals stood around, unsure of what to do.

"So what did you do to end up here in the hallway, Nell?" asked Clever.

Nell flapped a fin, revealing a long, lightning bolt–shaped scar on her side. "It's a long story," she said. "A story for another time."

Just then, everyone stopped talking. A rumbling sound was coming down the hallway. Suddenly Super Turbo came into view. He was rolling along at superspeed in his hamster ball. Wonder Pig was running to catch up with him.

Clever and Frank barely leaped out of the way as Turbo raced toward them, coming to an abrupt stop as he bounced off Warren's hard shell.

Dizzily, Turbo hopped out of the Turbomobile. "We can fill my Turbo-mobile with water, and Nell can ride along with us!"

Leo climbed down the wall he had scurried up. "I don't want to rain on your parade, Super Turbo, but there are holes in that hamster ball. The water will leak out."

"Yeah, but Boss Bunny, you have gum on your utility belt, right? We can chew it up and plug the holes," said Turbo.

Frank rubbed his whiskers. "That sounds almost crazy enough to work."

Clever turned to Nell. "Nell, what
do you think?"

Nell looked around at the other fish in her tank, then back at Turbo. "I like this guy! He's nuts! Let's do it!"

Working together, the animal superheroes put Super Turbo's plan into action. The classroom pets with buck teeth—and a lot of the animals had them—chewed up the gum. Clever used her beak to stick the chewed-up gum into every

hole. Warren noticed a bottle cap on the ground and calculated that it would take approximately 15.37 bottle caps of water to fill the Turbo-mobile. Leo scampered up the tank

and back down, carefully filling the bottle cap and then dumping the water into the Turbomobile.

Finally, the job was done. While the superpets held the ball steady, Nell leaped out of her tank and did a perfect triple somersault dive into the Turbomobile.

"Fantastic!" Leo clapped.

"Fantastic Fish! That can be your superhero name!" said Turbo excitedly.

"I like it!" said Nell as she swished her tail. "I'm not just Nell . . . I'm Fantastic Fish!"

6

SOMETHING *ELSE* SMELLS EVIL

They were all there. Super Turbo, Wonder Pig, the Great Gecko, the Green Winger, Professor Turtle, Boss Bunny, and Fantastic Fish. And they were ready to fight evil!

The only problem was ... what evil? The animals looked at one another, all clearly thinking the same thing.

"So . . . ," began Super Turbo.

"Um . . . ," said the Green Winger.

"Well, uh . . . ," added Boss Bunny.

"I'm hungry," said Professor Turtle.

"Great idea!" exclaimed the Great Gecko. "A snack! We're going to need fuel if we're planning to fight evil today."

The rest of the pets eagerly agreed. Then they crawled, scampered, hopped, flew, rolled, and otherwise walked through the doors of the empty Sunnyview Elementary cafeteria.

"Hold it!" Boss Bunny yelled. "I smell something rotten in here."

"Something rotten? Well, the school *is* closed because of the snow," the Great Gecko offered up. "Maybe they didn't have a chance to take out the trash."

Boss Bunny's pink nose twitched. "This isn't rotten garbage. This is a different smell."

"I don't smell anything," said Fantastic Fish. Although, to be fair, she was underwater.

"Yeah, Boss Bunny, how do you know what evil smells like?" asked Professor Turtle.

Suddenly Wonder Pig burst out laughing. "Boss Bunny, I'm pretty sure you're just hungry. We all are!"

The Great Gecko nodded. "Keep that nose to the ground," he told Boss Bunny. "I'm getting a snack!"

The other classroom pets ran off to the pantry, but Super Turbo hung back. Boss Bunny had seemed so sure there was evil afoot, but where? Who? WHAT? Turbo did one last scan of the cafeteria, then ran off to join his new pals.

By the time Super Turbo reached the other classroom pets, the pantry door was already open. The Great Gecko had scurried up the shelves, where he and the Green Winger threw snacks down to the others.

While everyone happily munched on chips, bagels, and crackers shaped oddly like Nell, Super Turbo noticed that Boss Bunny was still standing back, looking troubled. His nose was twitching more than ever. Super Turbo was starting to get the feeling that Boss Bunny was right. And that's when he saw it . . .

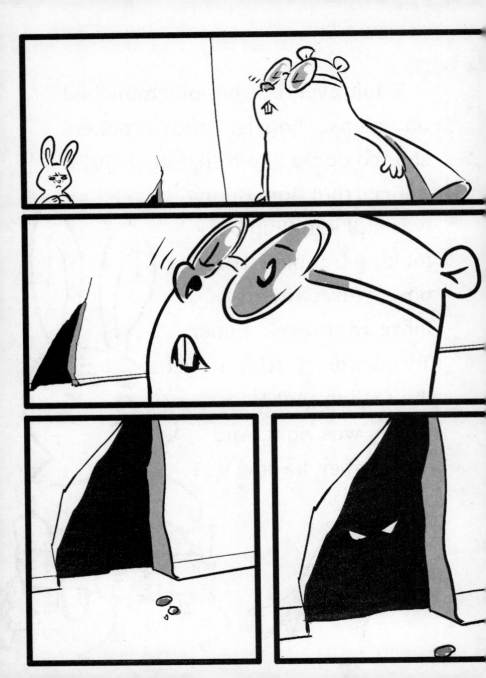

7

WHISKERFACE

A thin pink tail was sticking out of a hole in the wall.

It certainly has been a day for weird tails, Super Turbo thought.

Suddenly the tail disappeared. In its place a pair of beady yellow eyes stared out.

"Well, well, what do we have here?"

said a squeaky voice. A small hairy figure with big ears marched into the pantry.

Super Turbo stepped forward between this stranger and his new friends. He puffed out his chest and adjusted his goggles. "Stay back, Mr., uh . . . ," he paused, not sure what to call this creature.

"Whiskerface!" yelled the stranger.

"Mr. Whiskerface?" asked Turbo.

"I've been waiting for you all to arrive," Whiskerface said, sinisterly twirling his long whiskers. "You see, with all the classroom pets in one place, I can capture you and take over the school!" Whiskerface laughed a horrible, high-pitched laugh.

Before the super animals could respond, Whiskerface cried: "But wait! There's more! Because after I take over Sunnyview Elementary, I will use the school as my base . . . to take over the entire world!"

The pets blinked.

"I think you may have left out a few steps in that plan of yours," said Fantastic Fish.

"Enough distractions!" Whisker-face yelled. "The point is, I have you all where I want you. And now I will make you my prisoners!"

"Oh yeah?" said Wonder Pig, stepping forward. The *W* on her belly once again seemed to be *glowing*. "Well, look around. There's *one* of you and *seven* of us!"

Whiskerface gave a sly grin. "RAT PACK!" he suddenly commanded.

THE PLAN TO TAKE OVER THE WORLD

Through the hole in the wall, a stream of hairy, whiskered, big-eared creatures came pouring into the pantry. In seconds Super Turbo and the other classroom pets were surrounded. Super Turbo tightened his cape. This was it.

In seconds the entire pantry was consumed in an epic battle of good versus evil. Wonder Pig got behind Fantastic Fish and launched the Turbomobile forward. It rolled on a perfect path, scattering Rat Pack-ers like bowling pins. The Great

Gecko scampered back up on the table, where he and the Green Winger pelted the rats with grapes and ketchup packets. Boss Bunny climbed atop Professor Turtle's shell and fought off the Rat Packers with his eraser.

In the chaos Super Turbo saw an opening. He launched himself at Whiskerface and tackled the very

mouse-looking rat off of the bagel he was standing on. The two of them rolled around on the floor. Super Turbo's goggles were fogging up, and it was hard to see. When they cleared, he saw that Whiskerface had been stuffed *into* the bagel during the battle. And the evil rat was now wearing it like a tutu!

But at the same time, the tide had turned against the classroom pets. A group of Rat Packers was rolling the Turbomobile back and forth. Inside the bubble, Fantastic Fish looked like she was seasick.

Professor Turtle had retreated inside his own shell, and a couple of

laughing Rat Packers were playing catch with his visor.

Boss Bunny had been tied up with the string from his own utility belt.

A swarm of Rat Packers had cornered the Green Winger and prevented her from flying.

The Great Gecko had almost escaped by running up a wall, but a Rat Packer got lucky and caught the tip of his tail.

Even Wonder Pig, with her super-pig strength, was captured and down for the count.

Super Turbo suddenly realized that he was the only classroom pet left standing. The fate of his new friends, his school, and perhaps the entire WORLD depended on him!

9

WHEN HAMSTERS FLY!

Super Turbo had to come up with a plan. And fast! He scanned the pantry. The Rat Pack was distracted trying to keep his new friends from escaping. Meanwhile, Whiskerface *was* escaping. And that's when Super Turbo saw it.

Now, you know that a hamster

cannot fly. Maybe if you put a hamster in a catapult or something, you could call that flying. But that's not very nice. But on this day, against these enemies, well . . . guess what? Super Turbo flew!

With a thud, Super Turbo landed atop the table in the pantry. How long before the Rat Pack noticed him? The answer was . . . not long. Already they were racing after him.

Suddenly a lightbulb went on over Super Turbo's head. Well, it didn't go on, but it was there. And there was a long string hanging from it.

Super Turbo took a deep breath. He adjusted his goggles. He fluffed up his cape. And then with all the hamster speed he could muster, he ran as fast as he could to the edge of the table, leaped into the air, and

caught the string that hung from the
lightbulb.

KLANGALANGALANG!

The sound was unbearably loud.
Especially if you happened to be

a tiny little rodent with giant ears. Everyone knows rats hate loud noises! The evil Rat Packers fell down, clutching their ears.

Whiskerface, who was trapped in the bagel tutu, ordered his Rat Pack to cover his ears. But because of the fire alarm, the Rat Pack couldn't hear him. Instead they started crawling back through the hole in the wall. Seeing that he was deserted, Whiskerface turned and ran as well.

As he did, Super Turbo was pretty sure he heard Whiskerface yell, "I'll get you, Super Turbo! This isn't the last you'll see of me!"

THE SUPERPET SUPERHERO LEAGUE!

Later on, in the reading nook in the corner of Classroom C, the new friends gathered to talk about their exciting day.

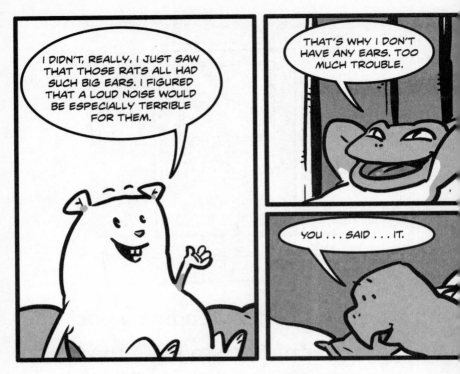

Angelina turned to Frank. "And I have to say, Frank, you definitely sniffed out that evil before any of us could. It's a good thing we have your super-smelling bunny nose to use from now on."

THANKS!

"Sunnyview is in good hands, thanks to us," said Warren, proudly.

All the pets smiled, content with themselves. All the pets but Leo. He frowned.

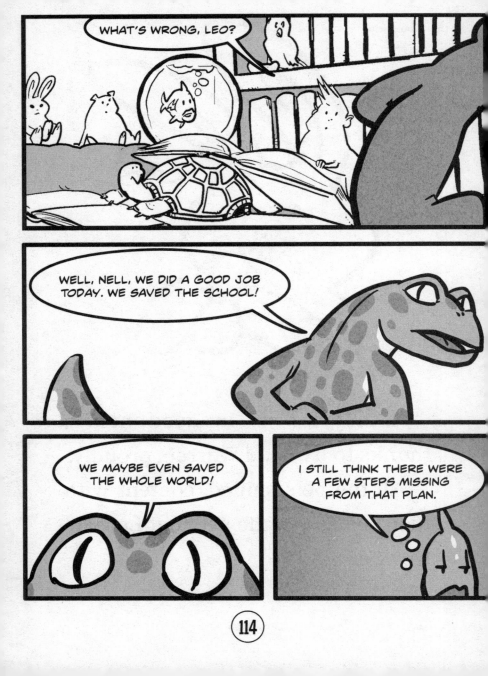

"Super!" shouted Clever.

"Pet!" yelled Nell.

"Superhero League!" cried Frank.

"And I propose that Classroom C, right here, be our meeting place," added Angelina.

All the animals agreed it was the perfect place for a team of superhero pets.

o   o   o

That night, Turbo returned to his comfy cage in the corner of Classroom C. He carefully folded up his Super Turbo gear and returned it to his secret hiding spot. He looked at

his hamster wheel, his hamster pellets, his water bottle.

Tomorrow, school would be back in session. For all the students, all the teachers, and even Principal Brickford, it would be no different from any other day. But it *would* be different. Because tomorrow, and forever after, Sunnyview Elementary was under the protection of . . .

Normally, Sunnyview Elementary was filled with kids and teachers and all the things that make up a school. But it was after hours. Everyone was at home or asleep. And not a creature was stirring, except for a—what is that? A mouse?

"Fellow rats!" a small, fuzzy creature with huge ears and long whiskers addressed a crowd of other creatures just like him. Although he was a bit smaller than the rest, his whiskers were longer. This is why he was called. . . Whiskerface!

"I suppose you're all wondering why I called you here tonight!" he continued.

There was a chorus of whispers. "Uh, was today Taco Tuesday?" asked a tiny voice from the back.

"No!" roared back Whiskerface. "It's not even Tuesday, it's Friday!"

"As you all know, the Rat Pack recently suffered a defeat at the paws of the Pampered Pets of Sunnyview Elementary."

Whiskerface stroked his whiskers as he reminded his Rat Pack what had happened.

A team of classroom pets had showed up in his cafeteria and halted his plan to take over Sunnyview Elementary and, eventually, the world!

"But as your fearless leader, I have taken steps to make sure that the Rat Pack will never be defeated again!" Whiskerface cried.